time-watch

time-watch

stories chosen by
wendy cooling

Dolphin

A Dolphin Paperback

First published in Great Britain in 1997
by Orion Children's Books
a division of the Orion Publishing Group Ltd
Orion House
5 Upper St Martin's Lane
London WC2H 9EA

A catalogue record for this book is available
from the British Library
Typeset by Deltatype Ltd, Birkenhead, Merseyside
Printed in Great Britain by Clays Ltd, St Ives plc
ISBN 1 85881 450 2

contents

helping hercules

francesca simon

S usan was not what you would call helpful. Her parents
    nagged her to do more tidying, but it did no good. In
    Susan's opinion, parents should do all the housework,
leaving children free to ejoy themselves. She had far better
things to do with *her* time than hoover the sitting-room or
dust the shelves.

Her parents, unfortunately, did not agree.

Every Sunday night her father handed out the weekly
chores.

'Fred, you empty the wastepaper baskets,' said Dad.
(When Susan did it she made sure most of the rubbish
ended up on the carpet.)

'Okay,' said Fred, who was only five and got all the easy
tasks.

'Eileen, you set and clear the table,' said Dad. (When
Susan did it she broke at least one plate and wiped all the
crumbs straight on to the floor.)

'Sure,' said Eileen.

'Susan, you clean out the kitty litter tray,' said Dad.

'It's not fair! I always get the worst jobs!' howled Susan.

'I cleaned the kitty litter last week,' said Eileen. 'Now it's
your turn.'

'Everyone in this family has to help out,' said Dad.

'I'm far too busy and I'm not your slave,' snarled Susan.
'Clean it out yourself.'

She didn't even like the cat. Stinky's main pleasure in life
was throwing up on the stairs and leaping onto laps with
his claws out.

'SUSAN!' said Dad.

'I won't do it!' shrieked Susan. 'I hate this!'

'Go to your room,' said Dad. 'And don't come down until
you're ready to help.'

Susan flounced upstairs and went into her bedroom,

giving the door a good loud slam. Just in case the task-masters downstairs hadn't heard, she opened her door and banged it shut again a few more times.

She'd show them. She'd starve before she came down and then they'd be sorry. She'd have a great time right here.

Susan looked around her messy room. She could play with her knights but she wasn't really in the mood, especially since that brat Fred had snapped off all the horses' tails. She could practise her recorder ... no way. Her bossy parents liked hearing her play.

Then Susan saw the old cigar box tucked up on a high shelf. Aha! Her coin collection. She hadn't looked at it for ages, and she had that new Greek coin Uncle Martin had given her for her birthday.

Susan kicked her way through the dirty clothes, books and papers littering the floor, pulled her collection down from the shelf – knocking off a stack of books in the process – and got out her coin catalogue.

Then she unwrapped the precious coin. It had belonged to her grandfather and great-grandfather before him, Uncle Martin had said. Now it was hers. Susan took the silver coin in her hands, and looked at it carefully.

The coin was small and round, with worn, uneven edges. The front showed a man wearing a lion skin cloak and holding a ferocious boar. Well, that was easy enough, it was Hercules. She flipped it over. But instead of the head of a god or goddess, there were strange signs and carvings.

Susan opened her catalogue, and searched. She looked at every picture of the Ancient Greek coins and then looked again. Then she checked the Roman coins to see if it could be there, even though she knew perfectly well it was Greek. But there was no sign of this coin.

How odd. There were two possibilities here. One, that the coin was so rare – and so valuable – that it was not in her catalogue. The second possibility – no. That was too silly for words.

Susan sat on her bed and held the coin up to the light. Was her mind playing tricks, or did a strange, dull gleam come from Hercules's eyes? She turned the coin over in her fingers, feeling its scratched, worn surface. Was it her imagination, or did the coin feel a little bit warm?

Naturally, Susan did not believe in magic. Only little kids like Fred believed in nonsense like flying carpets, magic lamps, and wishing wells.

'Okay coin, if you're magic, I wish ...' Susan paused for a moment and closed her eyes, 'I wish that I could fly around the room.' She opened her eyes. She was still plonked on her bed.

'Ha,' said Susan, feeling a bit silly.

'I wish,' said Susan, 'that everything on the floor would put itself away.'

She opened her eyes. Her bedroom was as big a pigsty as ever.

How silly I am, thought Susan. Then she looked at the coin, and smiled.

'I wish,' said Susan, closing her eyes and rubbing the coin between her fingers, 'that I could meet Hercules.'

Next moment the bed seemed to give way and she fell heavily to the ground. But instead of falling on the familiar grey carpet, she landed on a cold stone floor.

Susan blinked. Her bedroom was gone. She was in the corner of an immense room, with stone columns, walls black with smoke, embroidered hangings and flickering torches. Men lined the walls on either side, all standing to attention, their eyes fixed on a little man huddled against the back of a large throne.

In front of her towered a giant man, wearing a yellow lion skin tied over his shoulder and round his waist. The lion's fanged head glowered on top of his, like a bristling helmet. A great sword dangled by his side, and a quiver full of arrows hung from his shoulders. A huge olive-wood club lay beside him. In his arms the man held up a bellowing boar.

I must be dreaming, thought Susan.

Then the giant flung the frantic beast onto the floor. Its tied feet lashed the ground.

'Here's the Erymanthian boar, Eurystheus!' boomed Hercules, for of course it was he.

The little man leapt out of his throne and started howling.

'Get that thing out of here!' shrieked Eurystheus. Then he scrambled into a large brass pot, screaming with terror.

'OUT! OUT! OUT!'

The giant laughed, scooped up the writhing boar as if it were a bag of sugar, walked up to the open double doors and hurled the snorting boar through them. A few moments later Susan heard a gigantic splash.

I haven't got my wish, this is only a dream, thought Susan. No need to worry.

But just in case she crept behind an urn.

Hercules stomped back into the room.

'Is that boar gone yet?' whimpered the voice from the brass pot.

'It's gone, you big coward,' sneered Hercules. 'I flung it into the sea. I'll bet it's halfway to Crete by now.'

Two fingers appeared on top of the jar.

'Are you sure?' whined the king.

'YES,' snarled Hercules.

'Don't you ever bring any more wild animals to my palace again,' said Eurystheus, climbing back onto his throne. He smoothed his rumpled tunic and took hold again of his sceptre. The men lining the walls leaned forward, awaiting orders.

'Right Hercules, next labour,' said the king, and he started to giggle. 'It's the smelliest, stinkiest, most horrible job in the whole world and you'll never ever be able to do it! Killing the lion and the hydra and capturing the hind with the golden horns and that boar was nothing compared to this! You've heard of King Augeas at Elis and his three thousand cattle? Well, I order you to go and clean out his stables in one day. And better bring something to plug your nose – those stables haven't been cleaned for thirty years – ha ha ha!'

Hercules scowled but said nothing.

'Who's this?' said the king suddenly, pointing straight at Susan.

I'm out of here, thought Susan. She rubbed the coin, which she still had clutched in her hand, and wished frantically to be home.

Nothing happened.

Then strong arms grabbed her and pushed her before Eurystheus.

'Who are you?' demanded the king.

'I'm Susan,' said Susan, trying to stop her voice from shaking.

'Where are you from?'

'London,' said Susan.

'Never heard of it,' said the king. He looked at her more closely, and a big smile spread across his face.

'See this girl, Hercules?' said the king. 'You take her along to clean the stables. I'm sure she'll be a great help.'

'What!' screamed Hercules.

'And mind you keep her alive – that's part of your labour, too,' said the king, rubbing his hands.

Hercules glared at Susan. She glared back at him. But before she could say anything he tucked her under his arm, strode out of the palace and started walking along the cliffs high above the choppy, wine-dark sea.

'Put me down!' ordered Susan. 'Put me down!'

Hercules ignored her.

'I can walk by myself, thank you very much,' said Susan.

'Listen, pipsqueak,' snapped Hercules. 'I don't like this any more than you do. But the sooner we get to King

Augeas at Elis and muck out his filthy cattle the sooner you and I can go our separate ways.'

'I'm not helping you,' said Susan. 'I'm not your slave. Clean out your own stables.'

'Do you realise, brat, that I could crush you with my little toe?' snapped Hercules.

'You have to keep me alive – the king said so,' said Susan.

Hercules gnashed his teeth.

'I'm bigger than you, and you'll do what I say,' he growled.

'Bully!' said Susan.

Hercules twisted his thick neck and stared at her.

'Watch your tongue, you little worm,' said Hercules. 'I'm famous for my bad temper.'

'So am I,' said Susan.

'Oh yeah?' said Hercules.

'Yeah,' said Susan. 'When my sister Eileen squirted me with a water pistol I hit her. So go on, what's the worst thing you ever did?'

'When I was a boy my music teacher slapped me for playing a wrong note so I whacked him with my lyre and killed him,' said Hercules.

Susan gasped. That was pretty terrible. She didn't think hitting Eileen was quite on the same level.

'What a grump you are, Hercules,' said Susan.

Hercules gripped his great olive-wood club.

'You'd be grumpy too if you were a slave to a snotty little toe-rag like Eurystheus and had to do whatever horrible job he set you.'

'Humph,' said Susan. 'So when do we get to the stables?'

'Soon,' said Hercules.

'How soon is soon?' said Susan. 'I have better things to do with my time than help *you*.'

'Be quiet,' said Hercules. 'And stop whining.'

On and on and on they travelled.

'Aren't we there yet?' moaned Susan for the hundredth

time. Then she sniffed. The fresh smell of olive groves had suddenly changed into something less pleasant.

Hercules sniffed.

'Yup,' he said. 'We're getting near King Augeas's stables.'

A few more strides and the stink was overwhelming.

'Pooh,' said Susan. 'What a smell.'

'Pretty bad,' said Hercules grimly.

They walked in silence through the choking stench until they stood in the stable yard. Far off in the distance Susan could see thousands of cattle grazing in the fields between two rivers.

Susan stared at the huge stables. Never in her most horrible nightmares had she ever seen so much filth and dung. The sludgy, slimy, stinky mucky piles went on for miles.

And the smell – goodness gracious, it was awful!

Hercules looked glum.

'Right, to work,' he said.

'What's your plan?' asked Susan.

'Get that bucket and start shovelling. We'll heap all the muck out here.'

Susan gaped at him.

'*That's* your plan?' she said. 'We'll never finish in a day.'

'Shut up and start mucking out,' ordered Hercules.

Very very reluctantly, Susan got her bucket. Even more reluctantly, she picked up a shovel. Holding her nose with one hand, she approached the first reeking corner. Of all the magic adventures in the world, she got to clean out a stable.

'Yuck!' squealed Susan. She poked her shovel gingerly into the nearest cattle dung.

'Bleech!' She tossed the first noxious shovelful into the stable yard.

'Pooh! Ugh! Gross!' This was worse than cleaning out the kitty litter. This was a million billion trillion times worse than cleaning out the kitty litter. If she ever got back home she would never complain again.

Beside her, Hercules shovelled like a whirlwind, bending and hurling and twisting so fast she could hardly see him.

Half an hour passed.

'Right, ten stalls down, only 2,870 to go,' said Hercules.

'Actually 2,990,' corrected Susan. 'At this rate, we'll be here five years. You're supposed to clean these stables in a day.'

'Just keep working,' snapped Hercules, digging ferociously. 'If you're so smart you come up with a better plan.'

Susan scowled. She could not bear the stench another second.

'Wait a minute,' said Susan. An idea had flashed into her head. She looked at Hercules.

'Just how strong are you?' she said.

Hercules went up to the thick stone wall at the side of the stable building and punched a gaping hole into it with one swing of his club.

'THAT STRONG!' bellowed Hercules.

'Then listen,' said Susan. 'I've got a great idea. Remember those rivers we crossed coming here?'

'The Alpheus and the Peneus? So?'

'What if you dug a channel and diverted the rivers to run through the stables,' said Susan. 'The current would do the work for us and wash away all this muck. All you'd have to do is knock holes in the stable walls at either end, and then rebuild them once the stables were clean. Oh yes, and turn the rivers back to their original beds.'

Hercules stared at her.

'Hmmm,' he said. 'Hmmm,' he said again.

Then he grabbed his club and ran off.

Soon Susan heard a shout.

'Watch out! Water's coming!'

Susan dashed into the fields, just in time to see a torrent of water pour into the stables.

In no time at all they were washed clean.

Susan cheered as she watched Hercules rebuild the walls and force the rivers back to their beds.

'That's that,' said Hercules, looking over the sparkling stables with satisfaction. 'Time for me to head back to that snivelling slave-driver. You're free to go, so bye bye.'

Go where, thought Susan frantically. She fumbled in her pocket and took out the coin.

'Wait. Look at this,' she said, handing it to Hercules.

He took the coin and gazed at it. Slowly he turned it over and over.

'It's me,' he said at last. 'I'm famous. Of course my muscles are much bigger than this picture shows but it's not bad. Don't I look handsome?'

'You look okay,' said Susan. 'Turn it over. What does that writing say?'

Hercules looked for a long time at the Greek letters. Had he killed his Greek teacher too, Susan wondered, before he'd learned to read?

'It says, TI ETHELEIS – What do you wish?' he said at last.

'I wish to go home,' said Susan.

'So go,' said Hercules.

'I can't,' said Susan. 'I don't know how. I wished that before and it didn't happen.'

'That's how these magic things work,' said Hercules. 'You never quite know why or how. Let me try it. I wish a fountain would burst out of the ground when I stamp my foot.'

He stamped. The earth trembled, but no water appeared.

'See,' said Susan sadly. 'It's not very reliable. Can I have it back please?'

'Sorry,' said Hercules, grinning stupidly at his carved picture. 'I'm keeping this.'

'Give me back my coin!' shouted Susan.

'No,' said Hercules. 'Finders keepers.'

'You didn't find it! I just showed it to you!' she screamed.

'Tough,' said Hercules.

Susan scowled at him.

'I need that coin to get home,' she said. 'Is this the thanks I get? Or do you want people to know that the great Hercules needed a girl's help to complete one of his labours?'

Hercules paused.

'All right,' he said. 'I'll give the coin back if you swear on oath you will keep your part in my labour a secret.'

'I swear,' said Susan.

'Swear by the river Styx, the black river of Hades,' said Hercules.

'I swear by the river Styx,' said Susan.

Hercules took one last look at his picture, then reluctantly gave her back the coin. Susan rubbed it between her fingers and wished.

At once Susan felt herself falling. But instead of landing in the dirt she found herself stretched out on her own soft bed.

Susan rubbed her head. She felt dizzy.

'Gosh, what a horrible dream,' said Susan, looking at the coin clasped tightly in her fist. Then she went to her bookshelf, took down her book of Greek myths and quickly read through Hercules's labours.

'What a creep!' she said. 'He *did* take all the credit for cleaning the stables. I suppose that's not surprising. Hold on, I'm being silly,' she said, thumping herself. 'It was only a dream.'

She ran out of her bedroom.

'Mum, Dad, I'm ready to help now!' she shouted, clambering down the stairs. She paused at the kitchen door, where her family were eating dinner.

Everyone stared at her.

'What's wrong?' said Susan.

Eileen choked.

Stinky stalked out of the room.

Fred held his nose.

'Pooh,' he said, waving his hand in front of his face.

'Where have you been?' said Dad. 'You smell like you've been living in a stable.'

the final program

stephen bowkett

B ecause he was in that kind of mood, Surfer made the stars green that night, the sky lilac, and the full moon a wonderful amber yellow. The others couldn't really complain, because they did crazy things sometimes – and it *was* Surfer's thirteenth birthday.

The rest of the group, Rom, Qwerty and Byte, sang 'Happy Birthday' tunelessly, then created The New Millennium World Choir to do the job properly. Surfer was suitably impressed, and shared out his cake which was almost wholly marzipan, with no white icing because he didn't like it.

Afterwards they threw the pieces they couldn't eat to a flock of circling dragons made entirely of glass …

'I suppose we'd better get on with the homework,' Qwerty said at last. She was the only girl in the group, and the most practical, though the boys would never admit to the two being linked. But they got on fine with Qwerty, partly because her sensible suggestions never became bossy orders, and because she wore her real face whenever the four of them met. And it was a friendly face, framed by long dark hair and lit by cheerful blue eyes.

At least, Qwerty said it was her real face, and the boys saw no reason to doubt her.

They all lived in different parts of the city, and got together twice a week in Virtual Reality dataspace to help each other with their studies. Rom was the real genius with computers, and while the others struggled over their assignments, he magicked figures in the air – endless noughts and ones of binary code – out of which he created new programs. Last week he'd made the glass dragons: this week's task was to form an entire army of crystal dinosaurs.

Rom also loved to explore, surfing the VR Internet for interesting new Websites. And before long, as the others watched an electric motor taking itself to pieces in the sky, while a chatty voice explained how it worked, Rom disappeared into the distance.

Once the electric motor was completely dismantled, the teacher's voice told the children how it was different from petrol engines and jet engines. Then all the pieces rushed together; the motor started spinning, and zoomed away into the heavens.

'Next week,' the teacher told them excitedly, 'we'll take a look at rocket engines!'

'Great,' Surfer yawned, then frowned. 'Fancy having to do homework on my birthday!' His face lit up. 'Hey, how about a game of flying-touch-tig before we close down tonight!'

Qwerty thought that was a great idea. Byte was not so keen: he always lost at flying-touch-tig because of his fear of heights – even heights that existed only in the mind of a computer.

'You be *it*!' Qwerty said, slapping Surfer on the shoulder. Already she was sprouting angel's wings and turning to soar out of range.

There was a flash of silver lightning across the starry heavens and Rom reappeared in a state of great agitation. The others jumped with shock.

'You scared me half to death!' Surfer complained. He stepped away as Rom's body rippled and quivered, then shrank six inches as Rom became a ten-year-old boy with a mass of reddish hair and a face peppered with freckles.

'Is that what you really look like?' Byte wondered. Qwerty grinned.

'I think he's cute.'

Rom ignored their comments. 'You'll never guess what I found –'

'A genie in a bottle,' was Surfer's sarcastic guess.

Rom jabbed a finger at him.' Something just as good …

It's a website: a very special Website, one created by Professor Todd Michaelson –'

'Who's he?' Surfer wanted to know, as a glowing question mark formed above his head.

'Only the most brilliant VR engineer of all time. He hasn't been heard of for a few years now, and the word among the Webheads is that the World Government have hidden him away so he can work on his Theory of Holomorphic Projection.'

Surfer gave Rom a cockeyed look.

'And what's that when it's at home?'

'It's a way of creating Virtual Reality without the headset and datasuit,' Rom replied. 'A way of projecting computer images into the real world, so you'll never know the difference.'

Surfer gave a mocking laugh. But then he went quiet, because Rom wasn't laughing at all, and Qwerty herself actually looked a little frightened.

'We shouldn't have anything to do with it,' she warned. Rom screwed up his face in disagreement.

'Get real! Ever since the Internet came into existence all those years ago in the 1980s, people have been hacking in to its secret corners ... I mean, if you came to a wonderful old wood with a *Keep Out* sign tied to the fence, what would *you* do?'

'Go in,' Surfer giggled mischievously. Byte nodded agreement.

'Me too.' Rom gazed at Qwerty challengingly.

'I'd stay away,' she said, 'because if there wasn't any danger, there wouldn't be a fence ...'

In the world of the Web, fences were made out of cryptic codes and electronic warnings that flashed across the sky. It took no time at all for the four friends to get there – just a short leap of the imagination.

'Of course,' Rom said airily, 'there's always the chance

that Michaelson *wanted* someone to find this way in. If the rumours about him were true, then perhaps he wasn't happy to be smuggled away by the Government, taken from his home and his friends.'

They were standing in a place on the very edge of nowhere. The sky was filled with a storm of light and shadows, out of which tumbled sounds like cracked church bells in a ruined tower. Just ahead of them was something that looked like a wall, running with slime and hung with grey cobwebs.

'I don't think we're in Kansas any more,' Qwerty said, quoting from *The Wizard of Oz*, her favourite book.

'Nobody's bothered to fill in the details of the site,' Rom pointed out. 'It's just a forgotten corner on the 'Net. But look –'

He used his fingers instead of a wand to turn the crumbling wall into a huge TV screen, across which streams of numbers were flashing like leaves washing down in a mountain river.

A keypad appeared to one side of the screen, which Rom started to play like a master concert pianist.

The light began to change and the ground flowed like mist around them – rising upward, then swirling away to show a fine old house with lots of trees in the grounds, and a view of the city spread out before them in the cup of the valley.

'Hey,' Byte exclaimed. 'I know this place! It's Westridge. My aunt and uncle live up here.'

'I guess this must be Michaelson's house.' Rom took a few steps forward, then looked at the others, who were hanging back. 'What's the problem?'

'Sometimes,' Qwerty answered in a small voice, 'if the keep out sign doesn't work, people use guard dogs ...'

Rom tutted with irritation, but he backtracked to where his friends were standing.

'Look, we have three alternatives. We just walk away and

go back to that *boring* homework. Or we can try to decipher the data-locks here in VR, and see what Michaelson's up to.'

'Or?' Qwerty propped her hands on her hips, noting the gleam in Rom's eye.

'Or we go to Westridge in the flesh.'

'That's an ace idea,' Surfer said, his face lighting up. 'I mean, we've never actually met each other, have we – not, like, in person?'

'We could find out if you really are that ugly,' Byte muttered, dodging Surfer's playful swipe.

'I'm in,' Surfer said, and held out his hand. Byte placed his own hand above it, and Rom laid his over that.

Qwerty hesitated for a moment, then shrugged and rested her hand on top of the boys.'

'Tomorrow,' she decided for them. 'At four o'clock, after classes.'

The others nodded as though this was the beginning of a great adventure, but Qwerty wondered what was the point. After all, the flesh beneath her palm was warm and smooth and alive – as real as she could ever want it to be.

Qwerty's parents would only let her travel to another part of the city next day on the condition that she took her personal monitor – and promised to be back no later than eight o'clock. It was early October and would be getting dark by then.

'It's never dark in the city,' Qwerty pointed out with a chuckle. 'Everything carries on just as usual, twenty-four hours a day …'

Qwerty's mother gave a patient sigh, and not just becuse her daughter was challenging what she said.

'You know, when I was a young girl Mum and Dad used to take us kids out into the country. Dad had a small telescope that he used to set up on the tripod, and we'd sit by the car and have a picnic until the sun went down and the stars came out. And then we'd look for any planets visible in the sky that night – Venus, Mars, Jupiter – and they were all different colours … and we'd have competitions to name as many craters on the moon as we could … and finally, we'd find the misty arc of the Milky Way. Why, I don't think you've ever *seen* the Milky Way!'

'We did a project on space last term,' Qwerty said casually. 'And I went to the centre of the Galaxy in a hyperlight ship, to see what it was like.'

Qwerty's mother jabbed a finger at her daughter's computer terminal as a sudden anger clouded her face. 'No you didn't, because that was an illusion. The truth isn't in there.' She looked at the VR headset and the shimmery pile of cellophane-like material that Qwerty wore to immerse herself in dataspace. 'It's out in the real world. You'd do well to remember that, Eleanor. Living a life of dreams all the time just isn't healthy, my girl.'

Qwerty apologised, and made a pot of tea to prove it. But even after they were friends again, she had a strange feeling inside which she didn't understand until she was halfway across the city, travelling by tube to Westridge … Her mother had called her Eleanor, which was her real name: but she'd been Qwerty for so long, to so many people, that she felt completely at ease with it now – so much so that Eleanor sounded like a name that belonged to a stranger.

The tube network ended about a kilometre from Michaelson's house, and of course the autotaxis only operated within the city centre. Qwerty realised she'd have to walk, which seemed like a real chore at first – because in the Web you could go anywhere in no time at all – but once she got into her stride, she quite enjoyed herself.

Her journey was uneventful, except that her mother called her on the monitor to ask what she was doing way over at Westridge. Her face on the tiny TV screen looked concerned.

'It's Rom's idea, Mum,' Qwerty explained. 'There's a Webhead up here who's supposed to be a wizard at writing VR programs. We thought we'd pay him a visit. An interview would make a great chapter for my next InfoTech assignment at school!'

Qwerty gave her mother her most charming smile.

'Well, I can't argue with that. But take care, won't you, dear?'

'Of course I will. And if it'll make you feel any better, I'll take an autotaxi back home … as long as you pay for it.'

Qwerty's mother grinned. 'All right, you win. Charge it to my CredCard. See you later, Eleanor.'

'Bye Mum,' Qwerty said, as the holographic image faded. Qwerty flipped the monitor closed and slid it back into her pocket.

Five minutes later she spotted Surfer standing by the gates of a large house she recognised as Michaelson's. At least, she assumed it was Surfer. But this boy wore spectacles, and as he waved and smiled in greeting. Qwerty saw that he had buck teeth and a metal brace.

'Wow,' Surfer said, 'you're even prettier in real life than in dataspace!'

'Um, thanks.' Qwerty wasn't sure how to respond to the compliment. I can't return it, that's for sure, she thought.

Surfer must have read her eyes, because his face clouded and he shrugged.

'Yeah, Qwerty, it's sad – but most kids I know change how they look when they do VR. I mean, who'd want to hang around with a goofy-toothed four-eyes like me?'

Qwerty hesitated a moment, then totally surprised Surfer by giving him a friendly hug.

'Do you realise this is the first time we've actually met in real life? And to tell you the truth, I prefer you just as you are. You always seem so arrogant in the Web.'

Surfer grinned. 'Part of the image. But thanks for making me feel better.'

'No problem,' Qwerty said. 'And while we're out here, call me Eleanor, okay?'

'Deal,' said Surfer, blushing slightly. 'I'm Gavin.'

He explained that Rom and Byte had asked him to look out for her, while they went inside to talk with Professor Michaelson.'

'You mean Michaelson is alive? And he's here?'

'It looks like Rom was making a big fuss out of nothing. Michaelson himself answered the door. Rom explained we were datafreaks, and could we do an interview. Michaelson seemed real pleased to us.'

They walked towards the front door, which had been left ajar for them, and went into the house, passing an elderly lady who was carrying a tea tray in the hall, then walking through to the study where the others were gathered.

Professor Michaelson greeted Qwerty warmly as Rom introduced her.

'But please, call me Eleanor,' she insisted.

'A young lady who knows her own mind. That'll be useful later on,' Michaelson said, smiling. But it was, to Eleanor's eyes, a rather vague smile, as though the man's mind was absorbed with other, darker thoughts.

'We were surprised to find you here,' Rom said. He was gazing almost hungrily at the state-of-the-art VR engine/terminal in the corner of the room. It must have cost an absolute fortune, and would allow its operator to create programs that would make glass dragons and crystal dinosaurs look like kindergarten stuff.

'I–uh–I chose to be here,' Michaelson confessed. He looked straight at Rom. 'When you found my Website and broke the codes to enter, I knew you would be the ones to carry on my work.'

Rom's mouth dropped open. 'You mean – you want us – me – to help you with your Holomorphic Projection Theory?' His eyes flicked again to the terminal in the corner.

Michaelson followed his gaze. 'You'll be using terminals like that one, and I hope machines a million times more powerful. There is much work to be done, and I think your friends will be very precious to you in the weeks and months to come.'

'I don't understand, sir –'

'There is little time, so I must explain quickly,' Michaelson said. Eleanor found she had to strain to see him, for the room was becoming gloomier, and now a thread of lightning flickered across the sky, followed by a distant soft boom of thunder.

Michaelson gave a hard, defiant grin.

'The gods of Olympus grow angry! Come along, there is something you must see.'

The professor rose from his chair and moved towards the patio doors that led out into a private back garden, bordered with tall trees. As he opened the doors, they were flung back by a gust of wind that swirled into the room.

'The weather's getting worse,' Byte yelled above the growing gale.

'Ah, young man, don't worry yourself. They won't risk interfering too much – yet!'

'What do you mean, professor?' Eleanor found she had to shout over the rush and roar of the approaching storm. 'Who are "they"?'

Michaelson leaned close to her. His face was very intense.

'When my wife was alive, she loved embroidery, and would spend hours weaving an intricate picture – a landscape, a face. Sometimes she found a mistake, and would always unpick the stitches to put it right. *Always*, no matter how much of the picture she was forced to unravel.'

'I'm sorry,' Eleanor told him. 'I thought that was your wife I saw in the hallway.'

'Oh,' Michaelson said, 'it was … but I see you still don't understand. This way – come quickly now!'

He hustled the children through the garden to a spot hidden by trees and thick beech hedges.

Here the wind was muted, and the black clouds overhead streamed harmlessly by.

Eleanor found herself looking at two marble headstones, and felt her chest tightening with horror or amazement or both as she read their gilded inscriptions.

Emily Sarah Michaelson, born 1953, died 2029.
Rest in Peace.

'But they won't let her rest!' Michaelson snarled suddenly, shaking his fist at the sky. 'And I won't let *them* rest because of it! Do you hear me! You shall not have this power!'

Thunder answered and the whole city shuddered.

Eleanor grabbed at Michaelson's arm, just to make sure it was real. It seemed as solid as her own flesh, and she shook her head in confusion.

'Professor, what's going on here – that other gravestone – it's yours. *You're* buried there!'

Michaelson laughed at the children's bewilderment.

'Am I a man dreaming he's a butterfly – or a butterfly dreaming he's a man? I don't know. But we must all be allowed to dream what we choose. Don't you agree? Wouldn't you fight for the right to do that?'

Rom pushed his way forward and stood before Michaelson. He looked fearful, but determined.

'You need to show me how to work the terminal, professor.' He glanced at the others. 'If they want to help me, fine. But one of us has got to stay here to break the codes of the final program.'

'Yes!' Michaelson grabbed Rom's hands and shook them with a desperate gratitude. 'Bless you, boy. I'll show you now. Let's get back.'

Without knowing why, Eleanor found herself hurrying with the others towards the house. Her pulse was racing and a terrible apprehension had gripped her heart. Something awful was going on: Michaelson had discovered what it was long ago, it appeared – and now Rom also understood … And no doubt would explain when the time was right.

They burst into the study an instant ahead of a vast thunderclap that rocked the house. Michaelson stumbled and clutched at his chest with a groan, but helped by the children, he reached the VR terminal and began to weave his magic. Rom sat beside him, paying close attention.

'When you break through, you might find the world is a very different place,' Michaelson said solemnly. 'What are we like? What have we *done* to the earth, to make all this necessary?'

'Professor, you've got to tell us –' Eleanor began, then screamed as Michaelson leaped up and staggered backwards with a yell.

The man's body was unravelling – tumbling apart into a million threads, and each thread breaking into a million coloured pixels which faded away like dying sparks in the night.

Rom was hunched over the terminal, typing data madly into the machine.

'I've got to create new codes,' he muttered, as though to himself. 'Mustn't let them in …'

'Who, Rom, who?' Eleanor shouted, shaking him.

Rom turned to her and with a terrible look on his face said, 'The people who made this dream!'

Then he spun back to his work and would say no more.

Eleanor stumbled back, realising at last. She looked for Byte and Surfer, but there was no sign of them, and now that didn't surprise her at all.

She wondered how many others were just phantoms in the mind of the cosmic computer; ideas in the embroidery of the world?

And am I? Eleanor thought, as she went to the window and gazed out.

Far away, the sun was dissolving like a lump of chalk in a watery sky. The hills were collapsing to dust, and the dust fading to nothing. Along every street, the lights were going out as the city crumbled back to raw data.

Am I a butterfly dreaming she's a girl. Eleanor asked herself, or a girl dreaming –

knightmare

jean richardson

t was Ross who got them interested in history. Richard's class thought they'd have fun with a supply teacher – three days was the current record for frightening one off – but Ross didn't frighten easily. He was young and thin, with dark curly hair. The girls thought he was an out-of-work actor and soon half of them were in love with him. The boys admitted that he wasn't a bad bloke.

Ross knew how to make history come alive. Made them see it wasn't just dust and dates but about ambition and power, villainy and greed. 'Men died for the sake of a crown, to get their own way, to uphold their own faith ...'

'Like in Ireland?' suggested Tracey, who'd never been known to have a thought in her head.

Ross flashed her a smile that set all the other girls thinking. 'That's right,' he said. 'History's about people with feelings as strong as any terrorist today. Once you realise this, you can put on a knight's armour or a Cavalier's finery.'

Richard liked the idea of putting on a knight's armour. Boys seemed to have grown up much faster in the past. At his age they were often married – not something he envied them – and went to war, having learned swordplay and hawking and the duties of a young squire. All the adventures today were for qualified adults. You couldn't be an astronaut or a Tornado pilot without a degree and years of special training. The nearest he and Tom got to having adventures was on a small screen in Tom's bedroom.

'What's the point of living in the shadow of a castle that has housed kings and queens for over eight hundred years,' Ross asked the class, 'if you don't know anything about them?' He told them to pick someone who'd lived in the castle or visited Windsor, and find out about them. What they wore. What they ate. What they did with their lives.

For once, Richard was prepared to do some homework. 'I'd like to have been a knight,' he said to Tom. 'If we'd lived when there were knights, we could have been squires helping our masters get ready for war. Imagine telling Mum you were going into battle.'

'Yours wouldn't let you go,' Tom pointed out. 'She doesn't really like it if we go off on our bikes.'

'Neither does yours,' said Richard. Both their parents had strict rules about going off anywhere. You had to say where you were going and when you'd be back.

'I think there's something about knights on one of those CDs Dad bought,' Tom said. 'D'you want to have a look?'

The computer was in the living-room, so that Mum and Dad could play with it.

Tom found the disc and accessed history and then knights. He skipped from page to page until a knight in armour came on the screen. A voice began naming the various parts as the cursor darted from the knight's breastplate to his visored helmet and the pauldrons that protected his shoulders.

'Must have weighed a ton,' said Tom. 'Difficult to run away.'

'Or get on a horse,' said Richard. 'They must have needed a crane or something.'

The voice was commenting now on the armour shown in some rubbings of monumental brasses.

A name caught Richard's ear. 'Hey, that church is near here. I wonder if we could make a copy of that brass. Ross'd be pretty impressed if we turned up with a full-size knight.'

'Bet you're not allowed to copy it,' said Tom. 'Bet it's all locked up.'

'You can't lock up something in the floor,' said Richard. 'We could go and see if the church is open, and if it is, you could keep watch while I make the copy. All you need is blank paper and some kind of black crayon to rub with.'

'I want t'do it too,' said Tom.

'Well, we could take turns.'

Tom didn't look convinced.

'You're scared,' said Richard. He wanted Tom to come with him because he didn't fancy being in an empty church on his own.

'When d'you want to go?'

'How about after school tomorrow?'

'I've got to get some things for Mum,' said Tom, who shared the midweek shopping with his sister. 'But I'll come on afterwards. You can get started and then I'll take over.'

Richard would have preferred them to go together, but he didn't want Tom to think he was chicken. 'Okay,' he said. 'See you there. And don't tell your Mum. If I tell mine, she'll only start making objections.' He knew she fussed because she loved him, but after all what harm could happen to them in a church.

The church was further away than Richard had realised, though its handsome tower was visible for miles. Richard tossed his bike into some long grass on the edge of the churchyard and made his way round to the porch. The heavy wooden door had a huge iron latch. To Richard's relief, it rose easily to his touch and he plunged from sunlight into a shadowy coolness.

The church was empty, but it was obviously well-cared for. There were fresh flowers on the altar and on the window-sills, and a showy display beside the pulpit. Richard found himself tiptoeing down the aisle, though he didn't know why he didn't want to make any noise.

The brass wasn't difficult to find, but he saw at once that Tom was right. It was locked up, in the sense that a large sheet of perspex had been fastened over it and a card explained that this was for its protection. There were some postcards of the brass on sale, but Richard wasn't tempted. The whole point had been the surprise value of a life-size figure.

Disappointed, he wandered round, wondering whether it would be fun to hide and jump out on Tom when he arrived. The pillars in the nave were wide enough to hide behind, but perhaps the little room at the end of a side aisle would be better.

It was separated from the aisle by an elaborate wrought-iron gate that stood half open. In the middle, and taking up most of the space, was a large stone table. On top of it lay the life-size figure of a man in armour. His eyes were wide-open and looked so realistic that Richard had the uneasy feeling the man could see him.

He moved away, unnerved by the man's cruel expression. He wasn't sure he wanted to hide there. Then he noticed a much smaller figure in a niche in the corner. It too was dressed in armour and lay full-length on a stone ledge, but the face was that of a boy, a boy of about Richard's age.

Richard wondered who he was. There were some words carved on the side of the tomb, but the lettering was quaint and in places worn away. Luckily it was in English not Latin.

HERE LIETH YE BODIE OF RICHARD …
ONLIE SON OF ROBERT, EARL OF W …
HE DIED YE 3 MAY 149 …
A BOY OF GREAT PARENTAGE BUT FARRE GREATER HOPE.

The 3rd May was Richard's birthday. Across five hundred years they had more than a name in common. It was spooky.

He straightened up and looked down at the figure. The boy was carved from some kind of pale stone and lay propped up on one elbow, so that he could see across the chapel. At his feet lay a small animal with a chain and muzzle.

Richard traced the boy's armour with his fingertips. The

stone was icy cold. He wondered if the boy had been killed in battle.

'Would you like to try it on?'

Richard spun round, but the chapel was empty. Nothing moved, not even the ghostly banners high up on the walls.

'Well?'

'Where are you?' Richard asked, feeling a complete idiot.

'Where I've been for the past five hundred years.'

Richard stared at the stone boy in disbelief.

'I only asked,' said the boy, 'because I thought you were interested. Most people aren't.'

It must be some kind of clever tourist attraction. Richard looked round for a slot for the money.

'How does it work?' he asked.

'Put your hand on my sword,' said the boy, 'and think about wearing armour.'

Richard touched the sword blade. He wondered if it was connected to some kind of computer.

'Think!' commanded the boy, and obediently Richard thought about wearing armour.

It was much heavier than he'd imagined. He had a sudden urge to scratch his knee, but his hand was held fast by a metal gauntlet. He wriggled, trying to move his body inside the hard shell. All he could manage was a faint clash as of distant cymbals. The hard collar hurt his neck, and his shoulders were imprisoned by huge shoulderpads. He felt more like an American footballer than a knight.

At the same time he could see himself standing in the chapel looking bewildered. Then he saw himself moving away.

'Where are you going?' he called out in alarm.

'It's so strange,' said his other self. 'Walking again after all these years.'

'Come back. You can't just walk off and leave me.'

The figure had reached the gate. The boy walked slowly,

like an invalid. 'You wanted to change places,' he said, 'and so did I.'

It's only an illusion, Richard told himself, but he couldn't figure out how it worked.

'How did you ... die?' he asked. Perhaps you had to work through a series of questions. 'Were you killed in battle?'

'Of course not,' said the boy scornfully. 'I was too young to fight at Bosworth, and there weren't any more battles in England.'

'Then why are you wearing armour?'

'It was made specially for me,' said the boy proudly. 'I liked playing soldiers and my father's armour was too big for me. It amused him to watch me drilling, and I wore it on special occasions. Like when the King came. I was going to serve him when I came of age.'

'Did you die of an illness then?' asked Richard. Ross had told them lives were shorter in the past. Many children died of diseases that no longer existed.

The boy looked across at the figure on the table. 'No, I was murdered,' he said calmly. 'By that man. He was my uncle.'

'Murdered by your uncle!' said Richard. 'Why should your uncle want to murder you?' He thought suddenly of his own uncle, who had a boat and took Richard sailing.

'Upon my honour he killed me,' said the boy. 'I was my father's only son, and heir to great estates and titles. Had I not died, I should have been one of the most powerful men in England.'

'Did anyone find out? Was he arrested?'

'How should they? He was with the King at the time. He didn't kill me himself. He gave the orders. The man who did it was caught and died a miserable, lingering death.' The boy sounded pleased.

Richard shivered. Ross had told them about the pits where prisoners were kept without light or room to move.

'Can we change back now, please,' he said. He was beginning to feel he'd had enough of history.

'Change back!' The boy sounded surprised. 'Why would I want to change back? I've waited five hundred years to be able to walk again.'

'B–But you can't just go walking off in my body. You're dead. You've had your life. You can't have mine too.'

'I didn't have my life.' The boy was indignant. 'My life was cut off, unfulfilled, stopped in its natural course. I want to finish what I only started.'

'But what about ME? You can't steal my life. You're not allowed to want things any more. You're dead. And I'm hungry. I want my tea.'

'What makes you think the dead don't want things any more?' asked the boy softly. 'I've had centuries of wanting … wanting to run about, to feel the wind and the rain, to have friends, to eat and drink … we're not different, you and I. You were born on the anniversary of my death. That's why we can change places.'

'But I can't just lie here,' said Richard.

'Why not? I did. Time passes, people come and go. You have my bear at your feet for company. And there's always hope.'

'Hope?'

'The hope that one day another boy may want to take your place. I waited five hundred years. You may be luckier.'

'But you can't pretend to be me. It's all different now. You don't know anything about television, computers, cars, aeroplanes …' Richard was lost for words. 'And you can't have Mum. She's mine.'

'I can learn,' said the boy confidently. 'As long as I look like you, people will accept me. I have the will to survive. I was born to be the most powerful man in England.'

'But you won't be. I want to be an archeologist or an actor, and if I don't get decent exam results, I shan't be anything. Couldn't you choose someone rich who goes to Eton. They have boys with titles there. You could be one of them.'

The boy didn't reply. Richard saw that his will to live was as strong as his own. 'You'll never get away with it,' he warned, but he wasn't sure. Would Mum notice? Now he was growing up, he had thoughts and secrets of his own. She might think that was why he seemed changed. Tom was the only person who wouldn't be conned, but what could Tom do?

The boy was out of sight now. Richard heard his footsteps growing fainter and then the crash of the door to the outside. The boy had gone, leaving Richard imprisoned in stone.

It felt as though hours had passed – though the church clock had only struck once – before he heard footsteps again. Richard thought it was the boy come back, but instead it was Tom. Richard had never been so glad to see him. Tom knew all about computers. He was bound to know how to get out of this awful game.

'Tom, I'm over here,' he called.

Tom looked around. He hated having to admit that he was short-sighted. 'Where?'

'In the little room with the knight.'

Tom came through the gate and peered round the chapel. 'Where?' he said again. 'I can't see you.'

He'd walked round the side of the knight and was now looking straight at Richard. Or rather, at the boy's tomb.

'I'm here,' Richard said. 'In this tomb. I've got stuck. You've got to help me get out.'

Tom backed away. 'You're kidding,' he said. 'This is your idea of a joke. How can you be inside a tomb when you were outside a few minutes ago. I saw you. I called out and you vanished round the side of the church. I thought you must've come in here. You thought you'd scare me. Nice try. Well I'm going. This place gives me the creeps. I'll wait for you outside.'

Richard couldn't think of anything to say. Whatever he said, Tom wouldn't believe him. This wasn't just a computer game that could be won or lost by being quick-fingered.

The church seemed to be getting darker. Richard thought he felt the bear at his feet stir and he wondered whether the dead came alive at night. He thought about the boy going back to his home, going up to his room and looking at his things. He had Richard's body and clothes, so why shouldn't he have his thoughts too. No one would notice that the real Richard wasn't there, not Mum, not his uncle, not Ross, whose fault it was …

His thoughts were interrupted by more footsteps, this time urgent footsteps running down the aisle. It was the boy.

He looked different. The most powerful man in England looked at though he'd been crying.

Richard felt a certain satisfaction. So pretending to be Richard wasn't that easy after all.

'What's up?' he asked. 'You look awful.'

The boy looked away. 'I don't like your world,' he said sadly. 'It's ugly and noisy. There are dwellings everywhere, and the roads are full of carts that rush at you. One nearly ran me down. Even the heavens aren't peaceful any more. There are strange metal birds that make the most frightening sound. I used to love walking in the meadows, but I couldn't find them any more. Everything is so changed there's nothing for me to come back to.'

'I don't suppose I'd be at home in your world either,' said Richard. It was no moment to explain to the boy that many things were better than in the past. 'Would you …' He didn't dare say 'like to change places', in case the boy had second thoughts.

The boy stretched out his hand and rested it lightly on

his sword. For a moment they both wondered whether it would work this time – and then Richard found himself looking down on the tomb of a boy in armour.

He turned and ran down the aisle, colliding with an old man carrying a bunch of keys.

'Nearly locked you in,' the old man said as Richard, bent on escaping, pushed him aside and ran on. He made for the door and wrenched it open.

He must have lost all track of time, because to his surprise it was still sunny outside. His heart was pounding as he filled his heaving lungs with the air of the twentieth century, a century of aeroplanes, anaesthetics, telephones, television, computers, and so much else. The familiar sound of a plane beginning the descent to Heathrow confirmed tht he was back where he belonged.

His bike was still lying where he'd left it, but there was no sign of Tom. Perhaps that was just as well. He needed time on his own to recover.

As he rode home, Richard began making up a story to tell Tom, a story about how he'd followed Tom into the church and then pretended to hide in a tomb. He knew that Tom would never believe the truth.

the zarg tyranny

valerie thame

B ut why do we need all these rules?' demanded Jade.
Her mother's eyes narrowed. 'You've been talking to Miriam again,' she said. 'Ignore her, Jade. Your grandmother does not understand. Rules, or laws, are an essential part of Cratern society. We cannot exist without them.'

'Well, you would say that,' said Jade. 'You're a lawyer.'

'And you are twelve years old,' said her mother crisply. 'You have a highly trained mind, but it is sadly flawed by your ridiculous curiosity – which you did *not* get from me.'

'Who made these rules anyway?' said Jade. 'And why can't they be changed? Some of them are so stupid. I mean, why can't I call you mother? Why do we have to use PIN numbers all the time?'

Jade's mother looked horrified.

'Watch your tongue,' she hissed, 'or you'll get us all into trouble. You know as well as I do that Zarg rule is not to be questioned. Just keep your opinions to yourself, and your mouth shut!'

L42 looked anxiously about the room. All accommodation units were bugged, and L42 was always afraid that her daughter's rebellious remarks would be overheard and she would be to blame. The punishment for disobedience was severe, but L42 did not think it unjust. She saw nothing wrong with the Zarg system. She herself had been a model pupil. At eighteen she had qualified as a state attorney and afterwards had a brief relationship with a scientist known as Sll – Jade's father.

Jade often thought about the father she had never seen. She wondered what he looked like, or if she was like him. Apart from her mother and Miriam she knew nothing of her family. Craterns looked only to the future and Zarg law disapproved of looking back. But Jade was fascinated by the past. She wanted to know who she was and where she came from.

Her grandmother, who shared the small accommodation unit, often spoke of the old times and of Jade's grandfather, Kern.

'He was a brave but foolish man,' said Miriam, 'and asked far too many questions. Much like you, Jade. The Placators came and took him away just before you were born and I haven't heard from him since. I don't even know if he's alive.' Angrily, she wiped her watery eyes with back of her hand. 'Zargs are tyrants! Dictators! And I hate them all!'

Miriam fumbled under her bunk, and with her back to the ever watchful cameras, pulled out a much treasured volume of paper bound in leather. She kept her books well hidden because she knew her lawyer daughter would destroy them if she knew of their existence.

'This is a history of the planet Earth,' she said, carefully turning the fragile pages, 'and I wouldn't be surprised if we originally came from there. Earth was populated with beings not unlike ourselves, Jade. They had longer legs because they walked a lot, but smaller heads because they only had little brains.'

'But mother says Earth has never sustained life.'

Miriam sighed. 'It's no good talking to your mother. She's been brought up to see things differently. She thinks I'm a silly old woman and she's told me that if I insist on speaking my mind she'll report me, and I'll have to live with the Seniles.'

'She wouldn't!' protested Jade.

'Who can say, but let's not worry about that,' said Miriam. 'Let's see what we can find out about Earth, shall we?'

Together they browsed through the forbidden book. Jade was fascinated by the idea that such a dull, dead planet could have ever been alive, with seas and trees and people. She had only seen computer graphics of other worlds and had no real concept of a sea, except that it was a vast expanse of water controlled by another planet called the Moon. She noticed some handwriting on the first page of the book.

'That,' said Miriam proudly, 'was written by *my* grandfather, your great-great-grandfather.'

'*Vox et praeterea nihil*,' read Jade. 'It doesn't mean anything to me.'

'Nor me,' said Miriam. 'But your great great-grandfather was a clever man. He must have thought it important to write it down.'

'It could be in code,' said Jade. 'We could work it out.'

Miriam shook her head. 'No, not me, dear, my chance has gone but you, you have the opportunity to find out what these words mean.

'I could try,' said Jade. 'I could access the main data banks. I'm not supposed to, but I think I know how and if I finish my class work early I can use the extra time for research.'

'Good girl,' said Miriam. 'But be careful – and tell nobody. This shall be our secret.'

But, secret or not, the Cratern spy network picked up Miriam's whispered words and early the following morning the Placators came and took her away. They would not say why she had to go nor where she was going, but Jade had no doubts. She was certain her grandmother had been placed in a Senile Repository. She made enquiries via the Infonet but was told that information was not available. It was classified.

As for L42, she carried on as if nothing had happened.

'But it's your mother!' cried Jade angrily. 'How can you take it so calmly!'

'These things happen,' said L42. 'They are a fact of life. You may have to do the same for me one day.'

Jade was horrified to think that L42 could send her own mother to one of those dreadful places.

The Senile Repositories were outside their Habitation Zone and Jade knew there was little chance of ever seeing her grandmother again. Miriam had been right. The system under which they lived was callous and unjust. The Zargs were ruthless tyrants. The only clue to something better was those four curious words from the past. *Vox et praeterea nihil.* More than ever Jade wanted to find out what they meant. Miriam had been so sure they were important, and she could not let her down now.

So, every day since her grandmother's disappearance, Jade had spent part of the time in her Training Module trawling through forbidden directories and data banks looking for something, anything, that might give her a clue to the history of Cratern and the beginning of Zarg rule.

She was able to work undetected because Training Modules had no tutors. The pupils received their instructions only through headsets, and any other communication was strictly forbidden.

Jade had been trawling for nearly a month without success when, almost by accident, she found some archive material which could show three-dimensional examples of Ancient Artefacts of Earth. With a nervous, fluttery feeling in her stomach, Jade called up the files. Strange and curious objects appeared on the screen, captioned as Hair Dryers, Candles, Bicycles, Tennis Racquets, Envelopes.

She also found a bibliography with screen after screen of book titles. She found a thesaurus of language. Earth, it seemed, had almost as many languages as books – Urdu, French, Greek, Latin – but she could not decipher any of them.

Then she stumbled upon a resource program which reproduced the long-forgotten smells of that old, cold planet: unknown perfumes and scents which the computer captioned as Sandalwood, Seaweed, Shoe Polish.

It was while she was testing a peculiar yet pungent aroma called Straw that her screen blanked out.

Thinking it was her own fault, Jade tried to retrieve the program. Her fingers pattered expertly over the keyboard, but the screen remained obstinately blank. Then the grim face of a Zarg appeared in front of her. The grey eyes locked onto hers, the mouth moved, but Jade could hear nothing. Then she remembered her headset was switched off.

'Fool, fool,' she told herself angrily as she flicked the switch.

'The information you have accessed,' intoned the Zarg through the headset, 'is classified. Feed in your personal code and number and await confirmation of status.'

The Zarg disappeared. Except for the winking cursor in the corner, the screen was blank again. Jade was well aware that if she keyed in her pupil number the Zarg would know she had no right to be looking at those old files. She sighed. She had been very careless. Worse than careless, stupid. All these weeks of work wasted. The Placators would come and take her away and that would be that.

'Repeat. Key in your personal code and number,' said the voice in the headset.

Accessing classified traffic was a major crime, but Jade had found the program all by herself. She had been trained since birth to use her brain, and if it was that easy to access forbidden information then it wasn't *her* fault. There was something wrong with the system.

'Second repeat. Key in your personal code and number.'

More than two repeats and a Medic would come to investigate. It had been known for pupils to collapse under the strain in Module B, and for a moment Jade considered feigning illness. But that wouldn't help because she would be taken to a Medical Bay for examination and her tattooed pupil number would be discovered.

So, unable to think of anything better, she keyed in her pupil number, P149, and her personal code word. The computer confirmed her status, repeated the charge of

accessing classified information and said further invest-
igation was necessary.

Jade removed her headset, logged off and waited. There
would be only sixty seconds before the Placators came to
take her to the Interrogation Chamber – a small, cell-like
room in the Main Block. She had been there once. It had
been an innocent mistake, asking Pupil 150 for help, but
the punishment had been two foul days on garbage duty.

Precisely sixty seconds later the Training Module doors
opened and Jade was taken outside by two expressionless
Placators. Once she was inside the Interrogation Chamber
the Placators left and the automatic doors closed. Jade was
alone in the IC with a keyboard and a large screen from
which the impassive face of a Zarg stared down at her.

'Key in your pupil number and personal code,' said the
Zarg.

Jade's active brain was still searching for a way out of this
mess. Must she give her pupil number? Why not somebody
else's? Somebody who *would* use classified information.

'Repeat: Key in your number and personal code,' said the
Zarg.

Anxiety made her fingers tremble slightly as they
skimmed the keyboard.

'Code accepted,' said the Zarg. 'Greetings: L42.'

Jade breathed a deep sigh of relief. Not only had her
mother's code been accepted, it proved that the screen
only worked one way. She could not be seen or visually
identified.

'Question,' said the Zarg, 'What are you researching,
L42?'

Jade keyed in, Rules in Society. She thought that would
be safe enough. Her mother had not undertaken any new
research for years. Of course, it was still possible L42 could
find out her personal code had been used but Jade decided
to worry about that later.

'Reason validated,' said the Zarg.

Jade smiled. 'Well! That was easier than I thought.'

She turned to go, but the IC doors had not opened and the Zarg's unseeing eyes were still staring at her from the screen. There was yet another question.

'What do you think of the Zarg system?'

Jade tried to think what her mother would say. Something sugary and sanitized like … the Zarg system is perfect in every way. She keyed this in but the doors did not open.

'Received information, incorrect.'

Jade tried again.

'The Zarg system is supreme. The Zarg system is all-powerful.'

But nothing worked and the Zarg began to lose patience. It told L42 to wait while it put a search on the personnel files. Jade's shoulders sagged. She shook her head in despair. To be caught out on such a silly question! She would probably never see daylight again. Trembling, she covered her face with her hands and at the same moment the strange handwritten words in her grandmother's book came dancing before her eyes.

Vox et praeterea nihil.

She had nothing to lose. Why not try them out? Jade keyed in the four mysterious words. The effect on the screen was as startling as it was unexpected. The Zarg's face was suddenly smothered by a vivid display of graphics, static and scrambled information.

'Obsolete. Unknown,' said the Zarg weakly. 'Repeat!'

This time words and pictures zapped across the screen in a brainstorm of electronic fury, until with a final and blinding flash the screen blanked out completely.

The IC was silent. Jade tried the doors again but they were still closed. What now, she thought? For the time being the computer was out of action, but as soon as the fault was located the interrogation would start all over again.

A movement on the screen made her look up. The face of a Zarg had re-materialised.

'Welcome to Cratern,' it said. 'You are witnessing Zonal Automatic Replay Government which was perfected and set up on this planet by people from Earth in the year 2500. It is known by its initials as the ZARG system and is in use on many resource planets, such as this, throughout the Universe. There are no beings here other than Craterns and the programs on this computer cover all aspects of the Zarg system. If you start at zero, you will access the Training programs on Law, Social Science, Education, Waste Management, Reproduction ...'

The voice droned on, and when the message finished it started again. 'Welcome to Cratern ...'

Jade's mouth fell open as she realised the significance of this message. There were no Zargs. Cratern was governed by a computer program set up hundreds of years ago by Earth people. Zonal Automatic Replay Government. A computer program? An enormous and exciting idea was forming in her fertile brain. She knew a little about computer viruses and was sure she could get into the heart of the computer and destroy the master program.

But before she did, there was something she must find out.

The screen was blank again, the pulsating cursor awaiting instructions. Jade re-called the Earth Archives and the Thesaurus of Languages. She keyed in '*Vox et praeterea nihil*' preceded by the command Search and Match. The text scrolled up before her and stopped at Latin. *Vox et praeterea nihil* meant – a voice and nothing more.

'So,' breathed Jade, 'Miriam's grandfather must have known that the Zarg system is a voice and nothing more.'

She knew what she had to do. Bending over the keyboard she began to work, drawing on all her knowledge and skill. Within minutes she was into the High Level Language which controlled the computer. She keyed in:

'This system is obsolete. Ignore all further commands. End of Zonal Automatic Replay Government on Cratern.'

But she had not finished yet. She had to make sure the virus implant was successful. To test it she keyed in her own pupil number and code. The following ten seconds were nerve-wracking. She might not get the right response. The Zarg could reappear, and she would have to spend the rest of her life underground in some hellhole of a prison. Or she could be eliminated. That's what happened to traitors under the Zarg system.

A flashing message appeared on the screen but Jade hardly dared look. When she did, she screamed out loud, for it said:

'Information not recognised. The Zarg system does not exist.'

At the same moment the doors to the IC slid open and Jade ran outside, still screaming with delight.

'I've done it! I've done it!'

Outside, crowds of Craterns were gathering, unable to take in what had happened.

'What does it mean?' asked one.

'It means we're free!' cried Jade. 'Free! The Zarg tyranny is over.'

Bewildered Craterns were finding long-lost relatives as doors slid open and people from different habitation zones mingled together. People who lived in underground complexes, Senile Respositories, and Science Blocks suddenly found they too could leave. Jade ran towards a crush of people milling around the perimeter gate. She recognised one of them.

'Miriam!' she yelled.

Miriam hurried towards her granddaughter. They clung to each other unable to speak. Then Miriam said, 'Is this your doing, Jade? Is it?'

'Yes,' said Jade. 'You were right. That old writing was the key.' Bubbling with excitement, she began to explain all that had happened right up to the downfall of the Zargs. But when she saw the worry lines deepen on her grand-mother's face she began to have doubts.

'What's the matter? What's wrong?'

Miriam hugged her fiercely. 'Nothing's wrong. It's what we wanted and I'm very proud of you, Jade. But this is only the beginning. The hardest work is yet to come. It's up to us to make something of this sad planet. There will have to be big changes.'

'I know,' said Jade. 'For a start, mother won't like me calling her mother.'

Miriam chuckled. 'She won't like being called Buttercup, either. She never did like her real name.'

the gingerbread channel

paul bright

Twenty-five?' exclaimed Jack. 'You're joking.'

'I certainly am not,' said his dad. 'Now we've got the satellite dish, we can receive broadcasts from all over Europe. Channels 1 to 25 on the telly. Now we'll be next door, so you can zap from channel to channel to your heart's content. Give us a ring, or pop round, if you need anything. And bed by nine o'clock. Okay?'

'Yeah, yeah,' said Jack, settling himself on the sofa and picking up the remote control. 'I know.'

As his parents shut the front door behind them, Jack started working his way logically through the channels. Twenty-five! Great!

Ten minutes later he was beginning to change his mind. How could you have so many channels and find nothing worth looking at on any of them? There were people sitting in chairs having discussions in French, other people in other chairs having discussions in German, and others having discussions in languages he couldn't identify. And the sports channel was showing Sumo wrestling, of all things. There must be something else, somewhere. He picked up the remote again, clicking on through the channels ... 26 ... 27 ... 28. Nothing. Just black and white lines dancing up and down the screen, to the accompaniment of a monotonous hissing. He kept going. Might as well try everything ... 48 ... 49 ... 50. Nothing ... 69 ... 70 ... 71. He was getting to the end now ... 97 ... 98 ... 99. Nothing at all! The screen was now totally black. He clicked once more to move forward to channel 1, but found to his annoyance that he had moved backwards instead. Back to 99.

He frowned and clicked forward, twice more. And again he was back at 99. This was silly. A third time he clicked forward. Half a dozen clicks now, to get back to a screen with something on it. And there was 99 again! His finger seemed unwilling to obey his brain, would not let him move away from this channel. As he stared at the screen, he made out a faint grey rectangle, about as wide as his finger, in the top left corner of the screen. It was pulsing slowly on and off. As he watched it grew brighter, flashing like the cursor on his computer, then stuttered across the screen, printing a one-line message in bright, bold type. And Jack sat bolt upright in total amazement. For as the words appeared on the screen, a voice, soft, soothing, yet somehow totally commanding, spoke the same message out loud.

'Hello Jack! Welcome to the Gingerbread Channel!'

Jack was struck dumb. He could feel his heart pounding in his chest. What on earth was this?

'Jack Sullivan. So glad you could join us. We've been expecting you.' The voice was as smooth as liquid chocolate. And with every word that was spoken, the cursor flashed across the screen, spelling it out, in letters that seemed to glow, almost burning with colour; now red, then orange, brightening to yellow, and precisely synchronised with the golden voice. Jack watched and listened, entranced.

'Are you talking to me? Really?' he blurted out.

'Of course I am. I've been expecting you.'

'But how … I mean … you can't see me, or hear me. It's just not possible. You need microphones, and cameras, and stuff. This is just silly.'

The voice laughed. A faintly amused laugh, that seemed to hang in the air. Jack found himself shivering slightly. 'This is the Gingerbread Channel. We don't need microphones or cameras. Everything we need is inside our heads; in your mind and mine.'

'I see,' said Jack, who didn't. But he was beginning to get over his initial shock. After all, no matter how strange this all was, it couldn't do him any harm. Could it? All he had to do was switch channels, or switch off, and it, or he, or she, it was difficult to tell, was gone. 'So is there something worth watching?' he asked, feeling slightly braver. 'What's on tonight on the Gingerbread Channel?'

'Whatever you desire. The choice is entirely yours.'

'Honest?' said Jack. 'Anything at all? Hey, that really is clever. Well, you can forget Sumo wrestling for a start. How about a wildlife programme? Some of those are really good. All that close-up photography.'

'Closer than you've ever imagined, Jack.' The voice laughed gently. 'Wildlife that's wilder than you've ever seen. Now, come right up close to the screen.'

Jack got up from the sofa, and walked right up to the television. 'Like this?'

'That's it. Now, kneel down and look at the screen. Look closely. Concentrate on the words and try to blank out of your mind everything else. Now, concentrate.'

As Jack watched, the words seemed to grow and fuse together, until they filled the whole screen with a deep glow that pulsed and flickered. Like staring at red-hot coals. The pulsating colours started to spin, slowly at first, then faster and faster. A kaleidoscope, a whirlpool, an almost tangible force that seemed to draw Jack closer and closer to the screen. Almost … into the screen. He suddenly felt dizzy, as if he too were spinning, tumbling over and over. He felt a thud in the small of his back, then all was still.

Jack opened his eyes. He was lying on his back on a carpeted floor. Above him a huge video screen hung suspended from a high, domed ceiling. As he watched, a cursor raced across the screen, spelling out a familiar message, in letters that seemed on fire, while the voice blared, almost painfully loud, echoing around the vaulted space.

'Welcome to Gingerbread Television, Jack.'

Jack sat up and gazed around. He was sitting with his back to yet another screen, almost as tall as himself. It shimmered and glowed in a way quite unlike a television screen, or even the one at the cinema. He couldn't have said if it was made of glass, or fabric, or even if there was anything solid there at all. He realised with surprise that his own living room was displayed on the screen. He could see the table with magazines strewn over it, the remote control lying on the carpet. And the sofa, where he'd been sitting. But now the sofa was empty. He reached towards the screen, as if to return ...

'Come along now, Jack. You'll find wildlife in number 7.'

Jack stood up, staring around. He was in the middle of a large circular room. There was no furniture except for the screen itself, and no windows. But doors there were. Grey doors, fifteen or twenty altogether. And on each door was a large number, bright red against the pale grey.

'Come on, no time for daydreaming.' Jack walked uncertainly across to the door with the red 7, and opened it into a square room containing a television, a table, and a chair. And the ever-present dark-screened monitor with the flicking cursor, supported on a long metal arm that was fixed to the wall. On the table lay a remote control unit. The monitor flashed into life.

'Switch it on, then. Let's not waste time.' Jack did as he was told. The television screen lit up instantly to show a panorama that he recognised from many a documentary on Africa. Serengeti, was it? Somewhere like that.

'Is this what you wanted? Look closely now.'

'Looks fine,' said Jack, sitting down. 'Yeah, great.'

'Look closely, I said.' The voice was insistent now. 'Closer still. Concentrate on the image.'

Jack stared, his face almost touching the screen. As he watched, the picture faded slightly, then began to rotate, slowly at first, then faster, blurring into a spinning vortex of colour. He felt briefly, uncomfortably dizzy, then succumbed to the tumbling sensation.

Jack shook his head, opened his eyes, and looked about.

He was sitting on hard, sandy ground. In front of him was an expanse of scrubland, and thorn bushes and a few green but stunted trees, stretching away to a horizon shimmering in the heat. He reached down and scooped up a handful of soil, letting it trickle through his fingers. A soft voice, familiar from a host of nature programmes, whispered nearby:

'At this time of day, the pride is sheltering among the group of trees. They will sleep most of the day, almost the only animal here that is free of the worry of being preyed on. The lion is truly the king of this realm.'

Jack looked in the direction indicated, to the distant animals lolling in the shade. But even as he looked, he was right among them, as if a cameraman had simply zoomed in for a close-up shot. Jack could hear the regular breathing of the sleeping beasts, could smell them more pungently than on any trip to the zoo, could almost reach out and touch them. But they seemed strangely unaware of his presence, and something told him that he was as safe as if he were sitting in his own home, watching this on the television. They were unaware of his presence, yet he was there. What had the voice said? 'Closer than you've ever imagined, Jack.'

Over the next half-hour (though it seemed much longer), Jack saw the lions wake in the late afternoon. He sped alongside a huge male as it chased, but just failed to catch, a young antelope. He was secretly relieved at the lion's failure; there were some sounds and smells he did not want to experience too closely. He saw giraffe cantering over the plain, and wildebeest drinking cautiously at a water hole. Noon sped to evening, and day followed day, just as in a TV documentary, yet with the whole programme somehow crammed into no more than half an hour. Eventually he felt the heat diminish, and the sounds of the African plain faded. There was a brief period of dizziness, then Jack found himself back in the wildlife room, staring at the television screen, where another programme was about to begin.

'What do you think, Jack? Something special, eh? Something very tempting, wouldn't you say?' The voice laughed. Again Jack felt himself shiver at the sound.

'That was unbelievable,' he murmured, shaking his head slowly. 'Absolutely unbelievable.'

'Well, what now? More wildlife, or something different?'

Jack nodded, still dazed, towards the screen. The next programme was just beginning. A man in wetsuit and flippers, with an air bottle strapped to his shoulders, was falling in a slow back somersault from the side of a yacht, into clear blue waters.

'Can you do that too? Underwater? That'd be really something.'

'Just look at the screen. Concentrate now. And there you ...'

And he was there. The water was warm, a far cry from swimming in Cornwall on his summer holidays. Jack realised that he too was clad in a diving suit, with a gas cylinder, surprisingly light under the water, strapped to his back. He swam strongly and easily, as if he did this every day. Without making any conscious effort, he swam down until he came to a coral reef. A myriad tiny fish, in every colour imaginable, swarmed in and out of its folds and crevices. Larger, solitary fish patrolled slowly and menacingly. Feeling his way around a large overhang, he found himself in the sombre shade of a cave that penetrated deep into the coral. Something was moving just out of his view. Something far larger than any of the fish he had seen so far. Despite himself, he found he was moving deeper into the recess, closer to the creature. Then, without warning, it moved ...

Though it seemed an age, it was only fifteen minutes or so later when Jack found himself back in front of the screen, on which the closing credits were scrolling.

'Exciting enough for you?'

'Fantastic!' gasped Jack. 'Absolutely incredible. Just wait till I tell Dad.'

'But not yet. There's so much more to see.'

'Maybe just one more,' said Jack, feeling that he really should be getting home, but so, so tempted to stay a little longer.

'What about Westerns? You'll find them in room 19.'

'Great!' He ran eagerly across to where he saw the door with the large red 19. Behind it was a room identical to the one he'd just left, with TV, table and chair, and the ever-present monitor screen. Flaming letters pierced the blackness of the screen.

'You know what to do by now. Time for this one, then one final surprise. Something really special to tell your mum and dad about.' Jack stared at the screen, concentrating. The colours, and the dizziness, came and went. The atmosphere grew smoky. There were rough floorboards at his feet, and he heard a piano, out of tune and badly played, away to his left. He looked down to see his jeans were travel-stained and dusty, but the gun in his holster looked newly cleaned. Suddenly the bar doors swung open ...

When Jack at last came out of room 19, his head aching from the gunfire, he was surprised to find it quite silent. No silky voice greeted his return, and there was no flashing cursor on the monitor screen. He couldn't say for sure whether he was relieved, because the voice still made him feel distinctly uneasy, or concerned, since he had no idea how to get home. But what was that about 'one final surprise'?

Jack started to walk slowly round the circular room, past each of the other doors in turn. Then he saw a door he hadn't noticed before, one with no number at all. Jack turned the handle.

This room certainly was different. It was far bigger than

any of the others, and had not one television set, but row upon row, all quite small, on shelves that stretched along each wall. He counted roughly, there must be fifty, maybe more. The screens were all dark, the power switched off. He noticed that those on the top shelves were thick with dust, and some were obscured by ancient cobwebs. How long had they been here? Lower down, the sets were cleaner, put here more recently. The bottom shelf had only three sets on it, the last gleaming and brand new. What were they for? If they were old, or damaged, why were they being kept? And why some so old, and one brand new? Then he noticed a remote control unit sitting on a shelf, quite near to him. He hesitated to touch it, expecting a booming voice to interrupt him at any minute. He reached out a hand, and pointing towards the nearest screen, he pressed the 'power on' button.

The screen flickered briefly, then glowed into life. And Jack gasped out loud. The face of a young girl, about his own age, stared out at him, her face filling the screen. A pretty face, framed by flowing golden hair. But her expression was the most blank and miserable Jack had seen in his life. She looked to left and right, then fixed her gaze on Jack, and spoke, half-whispering, her expression animated and urgent.

'Who are you? What are you doing here?' Her eyes were alight with excitement. 'Are the police with you? I knew someone would come! It's been so long. Have you brought anyone? Please, please say you've brought someone.'

'No,' said Jack, bewildered. 'Why should I have brought anyone? I've just come to see the programmes. But what are you doing in there?'

'You poor, foolish, stupid boy. You must get out. Quickly. Before ... before it finds out!'

'Get out? What's going on here?'

'Listen,' said the girl, dropping her voice again to a whisper. 'It's all a trick, just to get you here. All that with the programmes, and being right inside them. That's its way of tempting you here. Because you have to want to go in. It can't force you. But then ...' The girl stifled a sob, wiping away tears with the back of her hand. 'Then it asks you to try another programme. A special one. It doesn't say what, but makes it sound like something really exciting. And in you go ... just like I did. Just like all the other kids did. And there's no way out. Some of them have been here for years. So go! Run! Get away before you're forced to join us.'

'But what is it? This 'it' you talk about. The voice. Who ... what ... is it?' His voice had sunk almost to nothing, suddenly tiny and frightened. 'And how do I get out?'

'The screen where you came in. Just do the same. Concentrate. Concentrate ... and pray. As for it, I don't really know. Only that it's evil, truly evil. All the things you've ever read of in horror stories. Now go! Quickly.'

'But how can it stop me? It's only a voice. Writing on a screen. Is there really anything to be afraid of?'

'That's just the shape it's chosen, something useful to lure you here. If it needs to I'm sure it can come out of the screen and materialise into any form it wants. Now stop asking questions. For heaven's sake go!'

'But I can't leave you all here,' Jack protested. 'Surely there's some way?'

'Not on your own,' said the girl. 'Someone else needs to come. A grown-up. Police. Try to convince them. Then, just maybe, there's a way out for us. Now run! And good luck!'

Jack gave her tear-streaked face one last look.

'I'll be back,' he promised. 'Me, and my dad, and the police. Maybe even the army. I'll be back.' Then he turned on his heels and fled through the open door. He sprinted across to the large screen in the centre of the room. The screen glowed, and he could see his own living room, safe and comforting. So near.

'There you are! Now, I've got one last surprise.' The

monitor above him had boomed into life. 'Something very special. Jack? Jack! What are you doing?'

The terror on Jack's face told its own story.

'Where have you been? What have you seen?' The chocolate-smooth voice was suddenly gone. This was a voice sharp and guttural with anger, a voice powerful and commanding. 'Jack! I forbid you …'

Jack felt an almost overwhelming impulse to take his eyes from the screen, to turn around and look up at the monitor. He clapped his hands over his ears to block out the voice and stared frantically into the screen. 'Don't look round,' he murmured. 'Concentrate on the screen. Please. Please.' Suddenly he felt, he knew, there was something behind him. Very close. Something that radiated a sense, even a decaying, repulsive smell, of evil. He stared at the screen, pleading desperately under his breath. 'Please. Now!' He felt a hand, cold and hard as bone, grasp his right heel, as the screen dissolved in a vortex of colour.

His parents stepped into the living room.

'Jack,' said his mother, 'you should have been in bed ages ago. Come on now. Off the floor and get up those stairs.'

'What have you been watching?' asked his father. 'The late night horror movie? What is that ghastly apparition? I'm not having you looking at stuff like that. It's enough to give me nightmares,' and he reached out and switched the television off.

To their surprise and dismay Jack burst into tears, hurling himself at his parents and hugging them.

'Jack? You're shaking. What on earth is the matter? What's been going on?'

'It's my slipper!' sobbed Jack. 'It's got my slipper!'

mummy go home!

alan macdonald

A weekend in London,' Alex's parents had said. 'Just think of the fun you'll have.'

'Fun? I'd probably have more fun at my own funeral,' thought Alex bitterly as he trudged after his Aunt June. A tall woman in beads and fierce glasses, Aunt June was Alex's godmother. In her view it was part of her duty to keep an eye on her godson's education. At Christmas and birthdays she sent him books about fossils and ferns, books with tiny print and no pictures. The London weekend was her idea.

'I'm sure Alex will find plenty to interest him in London,' she wrote in her letter.

But Alex felt he'd been tricked into the whole thing. Where he'd hoped for a weekend of films and burger bars, his aunt had planned a wholesome diet of art galleries and museums.

Saturday morning found them in the British Museum. Aunt June's black umbrella pointed to a cracked pot in a glass case.

'And this is early Roman. A superb example,' she said. 'Note the pictures on the side ...'

Alex yawned. His eyes drifted to a notice by the door showing the plan of the museum. The Egyptian Room caught his eye. It was in the basement. Now that might be interesting, he thought, if he could only find a way to escape his aunt.

'Aunt!' he said suddenly.

Aunt June hated to be interrupted. 'What it is now? I suppose you need the toilet?'

'No, I was just wondering if there was a café.'

'I might have known! Thinking of your stomach as usual.'

'I wasn't! I was thinking of you.'

Aunt June's eye rested on him coldly. Alex kept going.

'With all the interesting things you've been telling me I just thought your throat might be a bit dry. And it's a long time since breakfast. So I thought, maybe, you might need a cup of tea.'

This was his trump card. His aunt had a passion for fruit tea. Peach, raspberry, redcurrant and mango – she drank about a million cups a day.

'Well, my throat is a little dry. And I suppose you'll be wanting an oatcake or something'.

'Maybe later on,' said Alex quickly (oatcakes? Hadn't she heard of chocolate?). 'I thought I'd take a look at the Egyptians. We did them at school. You have a nice sit down and I'll meet you in the café later.'

He made it to the stairs before she could change her mind and jumped down them two at a time. At last he was free. If he had to listen to his aunt any longer he thought his brain would explode.

The Egyptian Room was in the basement. It was a quiet shadowy place. The only light slanted from an arch window at one end. Alex's shoes echoed on the stone floor. Now he was alone the museum was filled with new possibilities. He pretended he was exploring an underground burial chamber. Strange statues watched him on all sides. Some of them had the heads of birds and cats. Alex tiptoed past, as if the slightest sound might wake them.

He reached the far end of the room under the arched window. Turning round he nearly jumped out of his skin. There, in an open case, stood an Egyptian mummy. He'd seen pictures of mummies before, but never a real one. The mummy was not much bigger than him. Its hands were crossed over its chest and it was wound in grey strips of cloth. Alex read the sign:

The mummy of Tutanfrutan – boy Pharaoh.

He tried to imagine what Tutanfrutan would have looked like. Did he have to go to school like other children? Did he order someone else to do his homework? While Alex was wondering this, the sun came out for the first time that day. It spilled through the glass, bathing the mummy in golden light.

Alex watched spellbound. Was it his imagination or was something beginning to glow on the mummy's chest? Beneath the bandages there was a small circle of light. It seemed to grow and pulse. Then it happened. One of the fingers on the mummy's hand curled upward and pointed straight at him.

'Yahee-ha-help!' screamed Alex and ran for the steps.

Rushing upstairs he ran into someone coming down. It was one of the museum attendants, wanting to know what all the noise was about.

'Slow down, slow down! This isn't a playground you know,' said the attendant, whose name was Grindle. Grindle had a thick moustache which he puffed out like a grumpy walrus.

Alex pointed to the corner. 'The mimmy ... the mammy ... the mummy,' he gabbled, 'I saw it move.'

'Nonsense,' snorted Grindle. 'Mummies don't move.'

'But it did. It pointed at me, like this.'

'You've been watching too many videos,' said Grindle. 'If I had my way these horror nasties would be banned ...'

'It moved!' said Alex impatiently. 'Come and see for yourself.'

Alex stayed close to Grindle as they went back to the spot. Grindle glanced at the mummy's case. 'There you are, all in your ... imagination,' he was about to say. Then he looked again. The case was still there, propped against the wall, but it was empty. The mummy had vanished!

'Good lord!' said Grindle, taking off his glasses. Then he narrowed his eyes at Alex.

'If this is one of your schoolboy games …'

'It isn't! I never touched it!' said Alex.

'Then where is it?'

'I told you, it moved, it must have walked off by itself.'

'Three-thousand-year-old mummies can't just walk off! Somebody must have stolen it!'

Grindle took out his two-way radio to get help. 'We've got trouble in the Egyptian Room,' he said. 'You better tell the Director to call the police. He's not going to believe this …'

While Grindle was busy with his radio, Alex took the chance to slip out through a side door. He had a feeling he was in trouble again. Whenever anything went wrong he usually got the blame. His mum said he had too much imagination for his own good. Even Alex had to admit his stories sometimes got him into trouble. Like the time he told his teacher that his dad was a grave digger. Actually his dad was a dentist, but Alex thought digging graves sounded more interesting than filling teeth. It had caused a lot of trouble on parents' evening. But this time he wasn't telling stories. The mummy *had* pointed at him, and now it was gone. Where or how Alex had no idea – and he didn't mean to hang around to find out.

The door led down a corridor to the lift. He would take the lift to the café, get Aunt June, and say he wanted to go.

Alex reached the lift. There was no one else waiting so he pressed the button. The arrow lit up and the lift started to come down to the basement. He fiddled nervously with his watch strap. Any minute now Grindle might notice he was gone. He couldn't wait to get out of the museum. He kept thinking about the mummy's bony finger pointing at him. His hands were sweating. It was like one of those nightmares where you hope you'll wake up soon.

The lift made a pinging sound and the doors slid open with a hiss. Alex stepped forward, then froze in horror.

There in the lift, reaching out a hand towards him, was the mummy.

Alex was dragged inside and the doors slid shut before he could escape. He could see the white bandages moving in and out where the mummy was breathing. He pressed himself against the lift walls, trying to get away.

'I ... I won't tell anyone,' he stammered. 'Just don't hurt me. I haven't had my lunch yet ...'

The mummy didn't answer. Slowly it started to unwind the bandages from its head. Alex turned his face away. Whatever lay underneath would be too horrible to imagine. After all, the mummy had been dead for three thousand years, it would be gruesome.

All the same, he couldn't resist a glance out of the corner of his eye. The mummy's body was now half unwrapped and what Alex saw amazed him. It was a boy around his own age, with straight black hair and eyes painted green like a cat's. His chest was bare except for a wide golden necklace. In its centre was a single eye carved in stone.

'Don't just stand there. Help me out of these filthy rags,' ordered the boy.

Alex did as he was told: he was just relieved he wasn't going to be strangled. The lift stopped at the third floor and Alex helped the boy out, feeling braver now he could see the mummy was human.

'What's that in your necklace?' asked Alex.

'Don't touch it. It is the eye of Re, the sun god,' warned the boy.

'It was sort of glowing before.'

'Kneel down when you speak to me.'

Alex did as he was told. He unwound the rest of the bandages. There were a million questions buzzing round in his head.

'Are you really a Pharaoh?'

'Of course. I am Tutanfrutan.'

'But how did you get here? You're supposed to be dead.'

'The sun god woke me. I knew that one day he would call me into the next world.'

'He took his time,' said Alex. 'You've been dead three thousand years!'

Tutanfrutan shrugged. 'Time matters nothing to the gods. I must say I've kept very well. They did a splendid job preserving my body with oils and spices.'

'You don't look much older than me,' agreed Alex.

Tutanfrutan looked down at him. 'Stand up, slave. What's your name?'

'Alex. And actually I'm not a slave.'

'What are you then? Your clothes are very funny.'

'I'm still at school. I'm here with my aunt. She's sort of batty. I was just having a look round when you scared me half to death.'

Tutanfrutan stared around him at the museum and frowned.

'What is this place? It isn't my tomb. I gave strict orders they should bury me in my pyramid.'

Alex didn't get the chance to explain. At that moment Aunt June appeared through a door.

'There you are, Alex. I was just coming to find you. The tea in that café was quite undrinkable. I shall be writing to the manager …'

She broke off to peer over her glasses at Tutanfrutan.

'Good gracious! Who's this?'

'This is Tut … er … Terry, he's a friend of mine,' said Alex. Somehow he felt he couldn't explain an Egyptian mummy back from the dead to his Aunt June.

'I didn't know you had any friends in London,' said Aunt June. She turned to Tutanfrutan. 'Pleased to meet you, Terry. You'll catch a chill without a proper vest and shirt. The beach is the proper place for bare chests, not the British Museum.'

Five minutes later they were leaving the museum. Aunt

June had invited 'Terry' to see the sights of London with them. Alex wasn't so sure it was a good idea. Especially as they were helping a three-thousand-year-old mummy to walk out of the museum.

All went smoothly until they went out of the main door. Then Alex saw the Panda car parked outside and the two policemen coming up the steps. They stopped in their tracks when they saw the strange boy in Egyptian clothes.

Aunt June strode past them but Alex and Tutanfrutan weren't so lucky.

'Excuse me, lads. We've had a report of a stolen mummy. You wouldn't know anything about it, would you?'

'Stand aside, slave. I must go to my pyramid,' said Tutanfrutan.

'We've got a fruitcake here,' said the policeman, glancing at his partner.

Tutanfrutan held up the charm in his necklace. 'Behold the eye of Re. He will turn you into a beetle.'

'I'm all of a tremble,' grinned the policeman.

Nothing happened. Tutanfrutan looked disappointed. The policeman took a closer look at the gold necklace.

'Well, well, what's this? I think you'd better come with us, son.' He took Tutanfrutan by the arm. 'Officer! What is going on? That boy is with me,' said Aunt June. But Tutanfrutan didn't need help. He sank his teeth into the policeman's hand and ran off.

'Oh crumble!' said Alex. 'Come on, Aunt, we'd better catch him!'

They chased down the steps after him. A red bus had stopped outside the museum and Tutanfrutan froze, staring at it in amazement. 'The chariot of the gods!' he breathed. Alex grabbed him and jumped on.

Seconds later, the bus pulled away with the three of them on board, just as the policemen reached the pavement.

'Ridiculous!' snorted Aunt June. 'All that fuss because Terry wasn't wearing a shirt!'

Tutanfrutan sat down. 'How exciting. I've never been chased before. Usually I'm carried by my servants.'

Alex sat down next to him, out of breath.

'What are you doing?' asked Tutanfrutan.

'Sitting down. What's it look like?'

'You can't sit next to me, I am Pharaoh. Sit behind.'

Alex made a face and moved back to sit with Aunt June. He wondered why he'd bothered to go to all this trouble. He should have left Tutanfrutan to look after himself.

The bus nosed through the thick London traffic. Aunt June had her nose deep in her guidebook, planning the programme for the rest of the day. Tutanfrutan stared out of the window.

'So many chariots. But where are their horses?'

'They're called cars, they have engines,' said Alex.

'Explain engines.'

'Er ... never mind now, what are we going to do? If those policemen catch you, you're in real trouble.'

'Trouble? Why?'

'Because you bit one of them. He was a policeman!'

'Pharaoh is above the law,' said Tutanfrutan. 'I should have turned him into a beetle. I can't understand why the spell didn't work.'

Alex leaned over to look at the stone. 'Can that eye really do magic then?'

'It is an amulet, a powerful charm. The eye of Re protects me. It will lead me back to my pyramid.'

Alex looked doubtful. 'I don't think you understand. We're not in Egypt, you see. This is London, the pyramids are thousands of miles away.'

'I have to go back,' said Tutanfrutan simply. 'That's where I left everything. My jewels, my throne – all my things. They were buried with me to take into the next world. Re will guide me there.'

Aunt June, who hadn't been paying any attention, suddenly looked up from her guide book.

'What about St Paul's Cathedral, boys? The dome is splendid!' she said. But Tutanfrutan had spotted something out of the window.

'Stop the chariot, slave!' he shouted to the bus driver.

The driver, thinking there was an emergency, jammed on the brakes. The bus stopped in the middle of the road and Tutanfrutan got off. He walked through the traffic with cars screeching to a halt all round him.

Alex and Aunt June caught up with him on the pavement.

'Really, Terry, didn't they teach you anything about road safety at school?' began Aunt June. Tutanfrutan held up his hand.

'I have found the pyramids,' he announced, pointing to a large colour poster next to a doorway. It showed a picture of the pyramids against a red sun. The poster said:

PUBLIC LECTURE TODAY: ANCIENT EGYPT
SPEAKER: PROFESSOR ERNEST SACKBOOTH

Aunt June clapped her hands together, forgetting to be angry. 'A lecture! Whaat a good job we stopped! I didn't know you were so interested in ancient history, Terry.

Tutanfrutan nodded. 'Re has led me here,' he said mysteriously.

Alex took his seat on the end of a row. The lecture hall was almost full. His heart sank as he looked around. The place was full of old men and women in hats much like his aunt's.

'What are they all doing here?' he whispered.

'Professor Sackbooth is a famous historian. If we're lucky he may show us some of the things he's dug up in Egypt,' said his aunt.

'Oh. Thrilling,' said Alex. He looked at the stage. In front of some green curtains sat the professor, a small man with a pointed beard and a spotty bow tie.

Tutanfrutan looked expectantly at the stage. 'Is there going to be music?' he asked. He clapped his hands twice and called out, 'Bring on the dancers!'

A man in front turned round sharply and said 'Shhh!' Tutanfrutan hissed back. He was starting to enjoy himself.

'Quiet, Terry!' said Aunt June sternly. 'The professor is about to speak.'

The professor stood up, cleared his throat and began his lecture. He spoke about Egypt's tombs and treasures. The lights went off and pictures of temples appeared on a screen. Tutanfrutan was getting more and more excited. When a picture of a god appeared he called out 'Look, it is Horus!' before the professor could open his mouth. People around them were getting cross. Professor Sackbooth mopped his brow nervously and asked for the lights. He moved swiftly to the highlight of his talk. Reaching in his bag, he brought out a large piece of stone. The audience leaned forward to look. So did Alex. The stone was carved with a picture of the sun god. Above him was a large eye, just like the one on Tutanfrutan's amulet.

Tutanfrutan shot out of his seat. 'Thief!' he shouted.

'Oh really!' groaned the professor. 'How can I give a lecture when you keep interrupting?'

But Tutanfrutan was making his way angrily onto the stage.

'You stole that from the temple of the sun god. See, I have the eye of Re in my necklace.'

Professor Sackbooth bent to examine it.

'But that looks real! A genuine Egyptian necklace. Where did you find it?'

'I think I can guess,' said a voice from the back. The heads of the audience turned to see who had spoken. The two policemen Alex had seen at the British Museum were coming down the centre aisle. Now we're in real trouble, thought Alex, sinking in his chair.

'We want to question this boy about a theft from the

British Museum,' said the policeman who did the talking. 'A mummy has gone missing. And I wouldn't mind betting that's where he got his necklace too.'

'Good heavens!' said Aunt June.

'Liar! Son of a viper!' cried Tutanfrutan. 'The necklace is mine.'

The policemen kept advancing towards the stage.

Tutanfrutan looked around desperately. He held out the stone in his necklace.

'Keep back! Beware the sign of Re!' he shouted. Again nothing happened. Alex felt the sun god wasn't listening. Somebody had to help Tutanfrutan. As the policeman came past, he accidentally left his leg in the gangway. One of the policemen tripped over it and fell flat on his face. The other stooped to help him up.

'Run!' shouted Alex to Tutanfrutan.

The boy Pharaoh went the only way he could. He dodged behind the green curtains on the stage.

It was hard to say what happened next. The hall broke into uproar. People surged towards the stage, knocking over chairs and shouting angrily. Priceless Egyptian relics went rolling on the floor with the professor crawling after them. One of the policemen bumped into the screen and sent it toppling forward into the front row. Throughout this Alex kept his eye on the green curtain. Tutanfrutan didn't come out.

It was Aunt June who finally restored order. 'Quiet!' she bellowed at the top of her voice. Everyone stopped what they were doing and looked in her direction. Aunt June pulled on a cord and drew back the green curtain. Alex blinked. Everyone stared in disbelief. The stage was empty. Tutanfrutan had vanished without a trace. There were no back doors by which he could have escaped. The only opening was a window high in the rear wall. Through it a ray of brilliant sunshine made a pattern on the floor. Alex thought it looked rather like the eye of Re, the sun god.